To Ellen, Flo, and Marianne—
who undoubtedly would have taken the other worm
—M.C.

For Tom Feelings, to whom we all owe so much
—G.F.

Text copyright © 1972 by Mel Cebulash.
Illustrations copyright © 1993 by George Ford.
All rights reserved. Published by Scholastic Inc.
HELLO READER is a registered trademark of Scholastic Inc.
CARTWHEEL BOOKS is a trademark of Scholastic Inc.

Library of Congress Cataloging-in-Publication Data

Cebulash, Mel.
  Willie's wonderful pet / by Mel Cebulash ; illustrated by George Ford.
     p.   cm. — (Hello reader)
  Summary: Willie's unusual pet helps make the class Pet Day a success.
  ISBN 0-590-29062-2 (meets NASTA specifications)
  [1. Pets—Fiction.] I. Ford, George Cephas, ill. II. Title. III. Series.
PZ7.C2997W1   1993
[E]—dc20   91-44270
                                                                    CIP
                                                                    AC

7 8 9 10   09   00 99 98 97 96
Printed in the U.S.A

First Scholastic printing, March 1993

Willie's Wonderful Pet

by Mel Cebulash
Illustrated by George Ford

Hello Reader!

SCHOLASTIC INC.
New York   Toronto   London   Auckland   Syndey

Willie and Wendy were
in the same class.
And they lived in the same building.
One day Willie said, "Tomorrow is
Pet Day."

Wendy said, "Why did you say you would bring a pet? You don't have a pet."

"But I'm going to get a pet," Willie said. "I'm going to the park to get a worm.
Do you want to come with me?"
"Yes," Wendy said. "No one will have a pet worm."

That afternoon they went
to the park.
Willie found a worm.
He found two worms.

But he put one back.

Wendy didn't want it.

The next day many
boys and girls had
their pets in class.

Al had his dog.

Cathy had her cat.

Henry had his rabbit.

George had his goldfish.

Rita had her bird.

And Mike had his hamster.

Willie had a paper cup
filled with dirt.

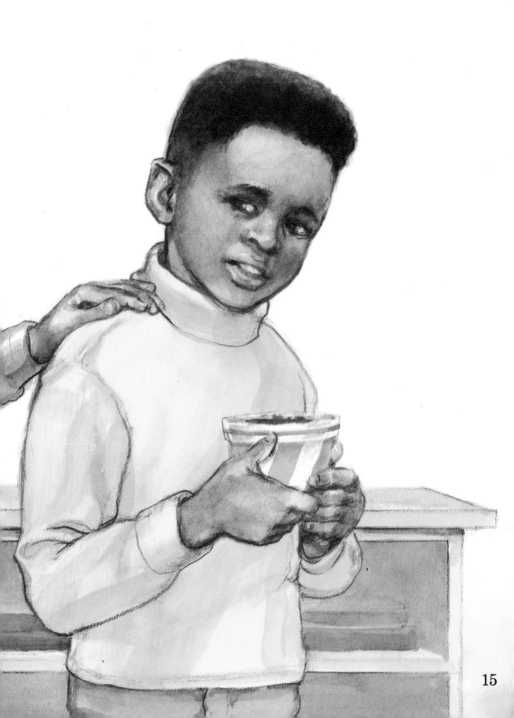

15

"What do you have, Willie?" Al asked.

"A worm," Willie said.

"What can he do?" asked Rita.

"I don't think he can do anything,"
Willie said.

"Then he's not a real pet," Mike said.

It was time for the pet show.

Miss Street said, "Willie, let us see your pet."

Willie showed his worm.

Miss Street asked, "What can he do?"

"Nothing," Willie said.

"I'm sure he can do something,"
Miss Street said. "You think about it."

Then Miss Street said, "Rita, what
can your pet do?"

"My bird can sing," said Rita.

But Rita's bird wouldn't sing.
And the other pets wouldn't do
anything.
Then Willie said, "I know! My worm
can crawl!"

Willie put his worm on the floor.

Everybody watched.

The little worm crawled and crawled.

Then...

Al's dog barked.

And Cathy's cat jumped.

Henry's rabbit hopped.

And George's goldfish came to the
top of the bowl.

Rita's bird sang.

And Mike's hamster ran around.

"Willie's pet can do more
than crawl," said Wendy.

"He can get things STARTED!"

THE END